SQUID ROW

Published by
Merry Publishing
12 Fenner Way
Chilmark, MA 02535
www.mvsecret.com

First Edition

ISBN 0-9761054-0-3

Book design by
Hawkins Creative Services, Inc.
Boston, MA
www.hawkinscreative.com

Printed by
Sherman Printing Co., Inc.
Canton, MA
www.shermanprinting.com

Illustrated, designed, and printed
in the Commonwealth of Massachusetts, USA

Illustration media, watercolor

Merrily B. Fenner

MERRILY B. FENNER, author, is a native of Martha's Vineyard, Massachusetts, where she still resides. Merrily attended Berkelee School of Music, 1963-65. She has played guitar and bass in local bands since 1960 when she joined her brother's jazz band. Merrily is co-owner of The Menemsha Galley and Gallery and is a Justice of the Peace. Her father, Hamilton Benz's life-long spontaneous storytelling inspired Merrily to create *The Secret* as a gift for her granddaughter Olivia in 2001.

Joan M. Walsh

JOAN M. WALSH, illustrator, was born and raised in Ireland. She studied at Dublin's National College of Art and Design, 1981–1985. In 1989, Joan moved to Martha's Vineyard in Massachusetts as a full-time artist. Joan's art graces the *Wampanoag Genealogical History of Martha's Vineyard*. She has self-published *Precious Moments on Martha's Vineyard*, written as an artistic personal insight into island life. As a Martha's Vineyard Preservation Trust commissioned artist, Joan painted the Flying Horses carousel in Oak Bluffs; her rendition now a collectable print.

Acknowledgements

To:

Larry Benz, my wise and wonderful brother;

Rick Fleury, supporter and dearest of friends;

Susan Klein, terrific editor;

Joan Walsh, brilliant illustrator who brought life to my story;

and to Frank, my incredible husband,

more thanks and love than you will ever know.

Merrily dedicates this book with love to her father

Hamilton Benz.

Joan dedicates this book to her family
on both sides of the Atlantic.

Eric was a happy boy who lived with his mother and father in a little fishing village called Menemsha. He and his big, black dog, Zippo fished in the summer on the wharf, walked around town and visited with friends along the way. Zippo was happiest when he was with Eric and looked forward to the ice cream they shared every day.

They were best buddies.

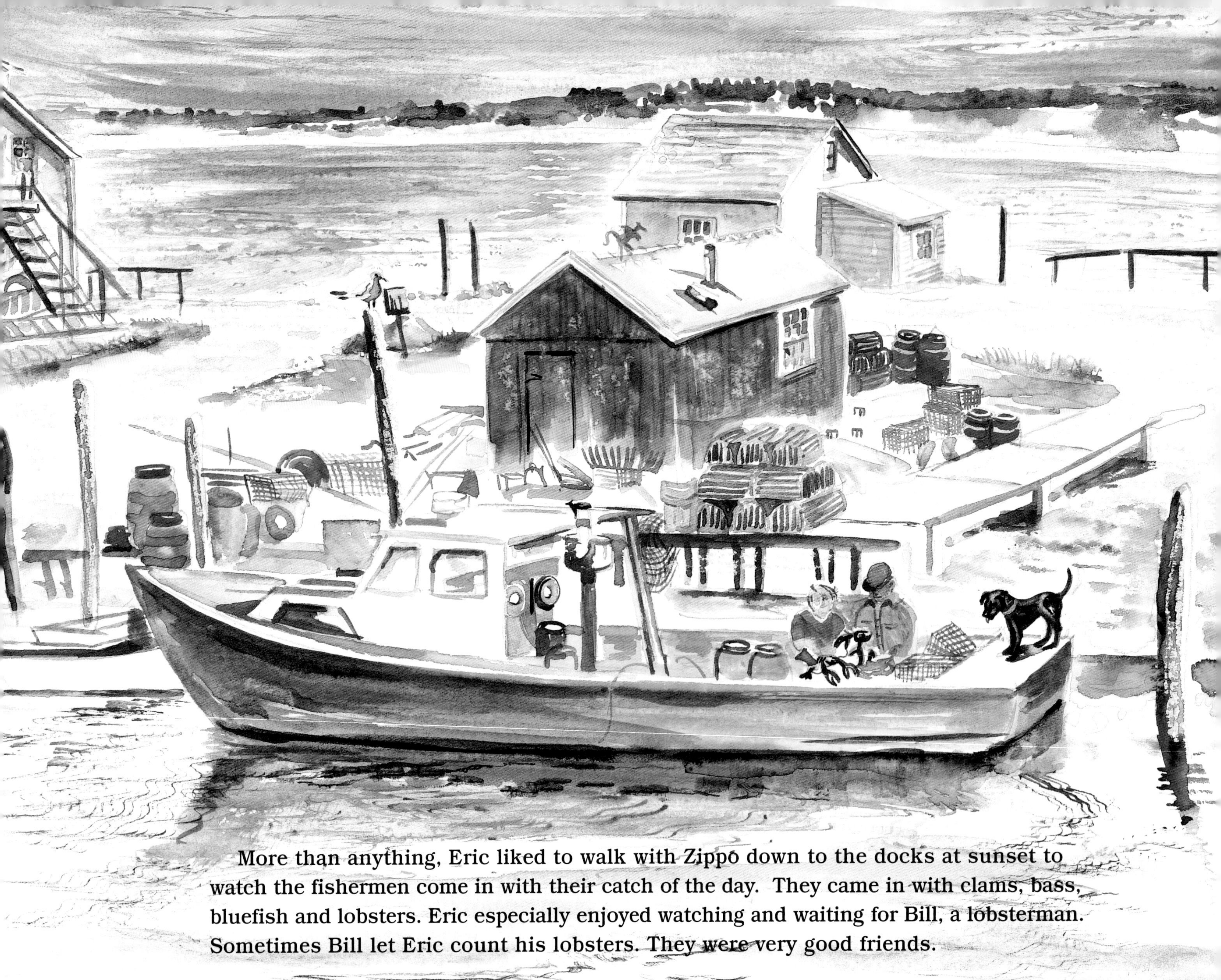

More than anything, Eric liked to walk with Zippo down to the docks at sunset to watch the fishermen come in with their catch of the day. They came in with clams, bass, bluefish and lobsters. Eric especially enjoyed watching and waiting for Bill, a lobsterman. Sometimes Bill let Eric count his lobsters. They were very good friends.

One morning Eric noticed that Zippo didn't want to eat and he didn't want to play. Eric pleaded with Zippo to come for a walk. But the dog's head was hanging low, his eyes were sad and drooping and he wasn't smiling anymore.

Eric knew Zippo was sick. Tears welled up in his eyes when he asked his mother what to do. She put her arm around her son and said, "Eric, it's important we get Zippo to the vet. He'll have the answer. Don't worry." They gently picked Zippo up and carried him to the car.

When they got to the doctor's office, the vet saw how sick Zippo was. He knew the dog needed some medicine to get better. So the doctor gave Eric's mother some pills for Zippo.

As soon as they got back to Eric's house they tried every way they could think of to get Zippo to take his pill. They put the pill on his tongue. He spit it out. They put the pill in his favorite food. He wouldn't eat. They put the pill in his water. He wouldn't drink. They were so upset. They didn't know who to ask for help. Eric's father was away on a trip so they couldn't ask him. Eric needed a plan and fast!

"I know!" cried Eric. "I'll go ask Bill. He'll help us!"

Before his mother could say a word, Eric was out the door, running as fast as he could — down the narrow dirt road, past the market, and over to the docks where Bill was working by his shack.

"Bill, Bill, you've got to help me!" he called. "I have a big problem!"

"What is it?" his old friend asked.

Eric told Bill all about Zippo. Bill thought a minute and then put his finger to his lips. "Shhhhh," said the old man. "Come with me. We're going to see a secret friend of mine."

"Who is it?" asked Eric.

"You'll find out soon enough," said Bill, with wide eyes.

Bill took Eric by the hand and rushed him into his red jeep, and in a flash they were driving around the bend heading into the hills of Chilmark. Eric asked about Bill's friend again.

"Be patient, Eric," said Bill. "We're almost there."

In the distance Eric saw a deep green sheep field with a pond in the middle.

They drove along a winding road through the meadow where sheep were eating grass.

When the sheep saw them, they bleated, “Baaaa, baaaa,” as if to say, ‘Hi.’
Big ones, small ones, black ones, white ones;
some baby lambs were hopping up and down. Up the hill they drove, and there,
at the tippity-top,
was an old abandoned well.

They parked the jeep by the field, jumped out, and raced to the edge of the old well. Bill lifted Eric to the top...

and . . . .

Hanging their heads over the huge black hole, Eric heard Bill sing with care to the darkness below. “Oh y-o-o-o h-o-o-o. It’s B-i-i-i-ll. I have a problem and I need your h-e-e-e-lp!”

They waited for an answer. Eric could feel cool air rising up from below. He wondered who on earth would be in a well.

He was getting scared.

"Are you in there?" cried Bill. They didn't hear a sound. Bill called out louder. This time he had a little shiver in his voice. "It's Bill! Pul-e-e-ze, please answer me! Are you in there?"

Eric listened carefully. From way down, deep came a low rumbling groan and then something scraped against the inside of the well.

"Whaaaa? Who's there?" a strange voice bellowed from below.

"It's Bill, and my friend Eric! Please, can you come up here?"

Eric was so frightened he could hardly breathe.

He couldn't believe what he saw
creeping up
from the deep,
dark
hole!

Two of the **largest** eyeballs in the world —
they were the size of footballs!

And then, there it was! The long, green face of a dragon! Eric was actually face-to-face with a real, live dragon who was smiling the sweetest smile he had ever seen!

"Heeeeeeey Bill, great to see you!" the dragon said.

"Eric," said Bill. "This is my secret friend."

The dragon smiled to greet Eric. Eric couldn't believe what was happening.

"What's up, my friend?" the dragon asked.

"Eric has a sick dog," Bill said in a hurry. "He won't take his pills to get better and we don't know what to do! I know you can help! You always have an answer!"

Eric watched and listened in awe as Bill and the dragon talked.

The dragon gradually stood up in his well as Eric and Bill stepped down and backed away. He moaned his low, dragon groan again and frowned as he was thinking. Just then, his eyes lit up and fire came streaming out of his big, round, steamy nostrils!

"oOOOOOo!" his voice rang out, as his eyebrows raised high with excitement. "I know a great trick! But you must remember that it only works for dogs!"

"What is it?" yelled Bill and Eric together.

Eric wasn't scared anymore. He was fascinated.

"What else?" cried the dragon. "Peanut butter!"

"Peanut butter? How does that work?" asked Eric.

"You'll see." the dragon said, and he leaned down into the well and pulled out a large jar of peanut butter. Pointing with his big claw, he said, "Now listen carefully. You scoop some peanut butter on the tip of your first finger like this."

The dragon dug into the jar with his claw to show them. "Then you put the pill in the glop of peanut butter, and you put that gooey finger into the dog's mouth, see, and scrape the peanut butter and pill onto the roof of his mouth....and bingo!" yelled the dragon with delight, as he happily licked the peanut butter off his paw.

"The dog will lick and lick until he swallows the whole pill with the peanut butter! I tell you," he said, with a huge smile and a big wink. "It'll work!"

Bill and Eric were smiling now too! They couldn't wait to get back to try the peanut butter trick on Zippo!

"Thank you, thank you! You're not just a dragon," Eric yelled. "You're the 'Peanut Butter Dragon!' That's just what you are!"

They all giggled at the thought, and Eric and Bill waved goodbye as they ran back to the jeep.

When they got back to Eric's house, poor Zippo was still so sick he could barely lift his head.
Eric ran to the cupboard to get the peanut butter and did just what the dragon had told him to do, as Eric's mother and Bill stood by. He scooped out some peanut butter. He put the pill in the glop of peanut butter on his finger, opened Zippo's mouth and scraped the peanut butter onto the roof of the dog's mouth.

And what do you suppose happened next?

Just like magic, Zippo licked and licked, and soon the peanut butter and the pill disappeared!

But now Zippo was very tired. He needed a nap, and Eric did too.

Bill wished them good luck as he left to go home. Eric lay down next to Zippo, and they both fell fast asleep on the dog's bed. His mother was glad to see the two of them finally resting and leaned over to give them each a kiss goodnight.

Very early in the morning when Zippo woke up, he raised his head, leaned over to Eric and licked him a big, wet kiss! Eric sat up with a jolt and saw that his dog was a little bit better. He gave him his morning pill in the peanut butter and the trick worked again like a charm.

Eric had to tell Bill the wonderful news before Bill left to go lobstering.

He nearly tripped over the dog as he ran out of the house and down the hill to the wharf. He was almost out of breath when he reached Bill to tell him that the trick was working. Zippo was getting better!

"He just gave me a great big kiss and he's even standing up! Oh Bill, I'm so happy!" cried Eric.

Bill leaned over and gave Eric a hug. "I'm very glad he's getting better," said Bill, with a smile. "I knew everything would work out fine, Eric. Our friend, the Peanut Butter Dragon, always comes through."

"Gee," Eric said. "What can I do to thank the Peanut Butter Dragon?"

"Well," said Bill. "Peanut butter is his favorite food. We'll bring him a brand new jar when I get home from work."

Late that afternoon when Zippo was feeling well enough to walk around, that's just what they did. Bill and Eric went to the market and bought the peanut butter to take to the dragon and this time Zippo went along with them.

Driving up the hill in the sheep field, Zippo was holding his head high in the air with the end of his nose moving back and forth, sniffing, sniffing, sniffing.

When they stopped, the three walked quickly to the well. Bill held Eric as they peered over the edge. Zippo was so scared! Bill called for the dragon and they heard that strange, scraping sound again, followed by a low groan. Then, out of the dark appeared the gigantic eyeballs!

Zippo was trembling. Ah, but when he saw the long, wonderful, sweet face, he wagged his tail as the enormous dragon climbed s-l-o-w-l-y up and **up** and **up** and out of the well.

"Zippo. This is the Peanut Butter Dragon. He saved your life by telling us to give you peanut butter."

The dog was a little shy at first. But the dragon leaned over with a beautiful smile to say 'Hi,' and Zippo licked his face to say 'thank you.'

Eric gave the dragon the peanut butter and oh, how that pleased the dragon!

And with that, they all joined hands as the dragon led them in a delightful circle-dance by the old well. The four of them were friends now. But what made them happiest was that Zippo was all better.

The secret friend, the Peanut Butter Dragon, had saved the day!

The End.